This book
belongs to:

_____

Disney·PIXAR
5-MINUTE STORIES

Written by Laura Driscoll

Illustrated by Ken Becker
and the
Disney Storybook Artists

Disney PRESS

New York

First Edition

1 2 3 4 5 6 7 8 9 10

Printed in the United States of America

ISBN 0-7868-3519-2

Library of Congress Catalog Card number: 2004112403

Visit www.disneybooks.com

Contents

· · · · · · · · · · · · · ·

Toy Story and Beyond!

A Tight Squeeze 4

Finding Nemo

Who's in Charge? 13

A Bug's Life

The Show Must Go On! 22

Monsters, Inc.

The Last Laugh 31

The Incredibles

Super Annoying! 40

Disney · PIXAR
TOY STORY AND BEYOND!

A Tight Squeeze

"Okay," Woody called to all the toys in Andy's room. "The coast is clear."

It was early one morning, and Andy had just left for school. He would be gone all day long, and the toys had the room to themselves.

"So, Woody," said Rex as the toys gathered in the center of the floor, "what's this game you were telling us about?"

Woody smiled. "It's called sardines," he replied. "It's like hide-and-seek, except the toy who's 'It' is the one who hides, and everyone else tries to find him or her."

Buzz scratched his head. "Well, what do you do when you find the hider?" he asked Woody.

"Oh, yeah," said Woody. "That's the fun part. When you find the hider, you hide with them and wait for someone else to find you both. Then, the next toy to find you hides with you, too, and so on, and so on. Get it?"

Most of the toys smiled and nodded at Woody. Bo Peep clapped her hands. "Ooh, this is going to be fun!" she cried.

But Jessie was still confused about one thing. "So, by the end of the game, everyone is hiding together in one spot?" she asked.

Woody nodded. "Right," he said, "except for the last toy who is still looking for the hiders. In the next game, that toy is 'It'—the one who hides!"

Now all the toys understood the rules and were ready to play!

"So let's decide who's 'It,'" Woody suggested. "I'm thinking of a number between one and one hundred. Whoever guesses closest to that number is 'It.'"

The toys took turns guessing. Woody was thinking of forty-nine. Hamm guessed forty-seven. He was the closest, so he was "It."

"Okay, everybody," Woody announced. "Close your eyes and count to twenty-five while Hamm hides."

The toys closed their eyes and began to count aloud: "One . . . two . . . three . . ."

Meanwhile, Hamm hurried away and started looking for a good hiding place. "Hmm . . ." he said to himself as he considered hiding inside Andy's toy chest. "Nah, too obvious. That's the first place they'd look."

"Ten . . . eleven . . . twelve . . ." the toys continued counting.

Hamm hurried over to Andy's bed and peeked under the dust ruffle. It was dark and dusty under the bed. "Nah," said Hamm. "Too scary. I'm not hiding under there all by myself."

"Eighteen . . . nineteen . . . twenty . . ." the toys counted off.

Hamm was running out of time! With only seconds to spare, he spotted one of Andy's old lunch boxes, raced over to it, hopped inside, and closed the lid.

"Whew!" he whispered to himself. "That was close, but I'm hidden!" Only then did Hamm realize that it was even darker inside the closed lunch box than it was under Andy's bed. "Huh," said Hamm, feeling slightly panicked but trying to keep his cool. "I, uh, wonder how long it'll take for someone to find me."

To his great relief, just one minute later, the lunch-box lid was lifted open and a Green Army Man peeked in. Upon spotting Hamm, he waved his battalion in. "Target located. Move, move, move!" he ordered as more Green Army Men scaled the side of the lunch box and rappelled down to Hamm's side.

Within seconds, they were all in and the lid was closed again.

"Hey, guys," Hamm said, glad to have company. "What took you so long?"

The next toy to open the lunch-box lid was Woody, whose eyes lit up when he saw Hamm and the Green Army Men inside. He glanced over his shoulder to make sure he wasn't being watched before he hopped inside the lunch box to join the hiders.

As soon as Woody was in and the lid was closed, he noticed that Hamm was standing very close to him. "Uh, Hamm," Woody said, "could you scooch over a little? I'm feeling a bit cramped."

"Gee, Woody," Hamm replied. "I'd like to help you out, but I'm already squished up against the sergeant, here." He pointed to the Green Army Man on the other side of him.

"Hmm . . ." said Woody. "This may become a problem."

Just then, the lid opened and Jessie peeked in. "Yippee!" she cried as she hopped inside the lunch box. "Found ya, didn't I?"

But there was no free floor space left inside the lunch box. Jessie got wedged between Hamm and Woody.

"Well, gosh, boys," said Jessie. "It's a little bit crowded in here, isn't it?"

The situation only got worse as more and more toys found the hiders.

Slinky Dog only managed to fit inside by standing over a Green Army Man.

"Ow, your paw is in my ear," the Green Army Man told Slinky Dog.

Buzz heard the toys complaining and located the hiding place. "Make way, folks!" he exclaimed as he piled in. But as hard as he tried, he couldn't get the lid to close.

By the time Rex found the hiders, there was absolutely no way he could even climb in.

"Hey, no fair!" Rex exclaimed. "I found you guys, but there's no room for me to hide with you. What do I do now, Woody?"

"Shhhh!" Woody said, raising a finger to his lips. "Keep your voice down or everyone will come over and see where we're hiding."

But it was too late. The rest of the toys were already hurrying over to the overstuffed lunch box.

"Oh, well," said Woody with a laugh. "Everyone has found us, so this game is over. Everybody out!"

One by one, the toys tumbled out of the lunch box and gathered around Hamm. "Gosh, Hamm, couldn't you have picked a bigger hiding place?" Rex asked him.

Hamm's cheeks blushed red as all the toys waited for an answer. Then, thinking quickly, Hamm replied, "Well, yeah, but isn't the point of the game to get squished? Like sardines in a can? The game *is* called sardines, isn't it?"

The toys thought that over and had to agree. "You've got a point there, Hamm," said Buzz.

And from then on, every time the toys played sardines, the hider made sure to pick a small hiding place—just to keep things interesting!

Who's in Charge?

"Now, Dory," said Marlin, "are you *sure* you can handle watching Nemo for a little while this afternoon? I just have a few errands to run, and I'll only be a couple of hours. But you have to *promise* you'll keep a close eye on him. Can you do that?"

Outside Marlin and Nemo's anemone home, Marlin darted this way and that, "pacing" anxiously, while Dory and Nemo calmly looked on.

"I can do that!" Dory replied confidently.

"We'll be fine, Dad," Nemo said. "Don't worry."

But Marlin *was* a little worried. It was a simple fact that Dory forgot things—often, important things. And there were three things that Nemo needed to get done that afternoon.

"Now remember, both of you," Marlin instructed them, "while I'm gone, Nemo needs to do his science homework, practice playing his conch shell, and clean the anemone. Okay, say that back to me."

"Nemo needs to . . . um . . . oh, it's right at the tip of my tongue," Dory said.

"Science homework, conch shell, clean the anemone," said Nemo. "I got it, Dad. No problem."

"That's right! What he said," Dory agreed.

Finally, Marlin waved good-bye and swam off to do his errands.

As soon as he was gone, Dory began swimming in circles around the anemone.

"Hee, hee, hee!" she laughed as she raced around and around. "Nemo, betcha can't catch me! No way! 'Cause you're too slow. . . ."

Nemo raced off, chasing Dory around the anemone a few times. It was fun, and Nemo wished they could play all afternoon. But he knew they couldn't. So he stopped chasing Dory and tried to get her attention.

"Dory, come on," Nemo called to her. "That was fun, but now I'd better get started on my science homework."

Dory swam over. "Your science homework?" she said as she tried to catch her breath. "Aw, can't you do that tomorrow?"

Nemo shook his head. "Like my dad said, I have to do it this afternoon," he explained. "It's due tomorrow."

Nemo explained his assignment to Dory: he had to find a sand dollar to bring into class the next day.

So Nemo and Dory swam around the reef, looking for a sand dollar. Before long, Nemo spotted one lying on the seafloor under a coral outcropping. He picked it up gently.

"I found one!" Nemo exclaimed.

"That's great!" replied Dory. "Now we can play!"

But Nemo reminded her about their to-do list. "No, Dory," he said. "Now I need to practice playing my conch shell."

"You do?" said Dory, sounding disappointed.

Nemo sighed. "Didn't you hear my dad say that?" he asked. "I have band practice tomorrow at school."

"Oh," Dory said with a shrug. "That's news to me, but all right."

They swam back to the anemone, where Nemo put his sand dollar away and got out his conch shell. He had Dory keep time while he played the songs that he needed to memorize for band practice.

"Yeah, play it, Nico!" Dory exclaimed as she grooved to the tunes.

Nemo played and played and played until he felt ready for band practice the next day.

"Thanks, Dory!" he said at last. "We're done."

"Yippee!" Dory shouted, swimming excitedly around Nemo. "Now it's playtime!"

But Nemo remembered their work wasn't done yet. "Not quite, Dory," he said. "I have to clean the anemone before I can play."

"Clean?" Dory said with a frustrated sigh. "On a beautiful afternoon like this?"

Nemo shrugged. "Dad said I should do it before he got home," he replied.

Together, Dory and Nemo cleaned up the zooplankton crumbs that were cluttering the anemone. It only took a few minutes, but when they were finished, the place was spotless.

"Thanks for helping me, Dory," said Nemo. "That went fast with the two of us working together."

"You're welcome," Dory replied. "So, what do you want to do now?"

Nemo laughed. "What do I want to do *now*?" he echoed. "I want to play!"

"Play, huh?" Dory said, weighing the idea as if it had never crossed her mind. "Now, *that's* a crazy idea. I like it!"

So Nemo and Dory played tag. Now and then, Dory forgot who was "It" and wound up getting tagged while she stopped to think. Even so, they had a lot of fun chasing each other until Marlin got home.

"Hi, Dad!" Nemo greeted him.

"Hey, Nemo!" Marlin replied. "Hi, Dory. How was your afternoon?"

"Great!" Dory cried.

"Yeah, great!" Nemo agreed. "I did my science home-work, practiced my conch shell, and cleaned the anemone. And we even had time to play!"

Marlin looked impressed. "Wow," he said. Then he turned to Dory. "Good job, Dory. Thanks for watching Nemo and making sure he got everything done. I really appreciate it."

"Aw, don't mention it," Dory replied humbly.

Nemo couldn't believe it! All afternoon, all Dory had wanted to do was play. It was Nemo who had reminded *her* about the things he needed to get done. And now his dad was giving Dory all the credit?

"But, Dad . . ." Nemo started to object.

Marlin looked over at Nemo and gave him a knowing wink—and Nemo understood. His dad *did* know the truth, and he was very proud of Nemo.

And that was all the credit Nemo needed.

"Yeah, Dory," said Nemo, patting her on the back. "You're good at being in charge."

The Show Must Go On!

"Flik, long time no see!" cried Rosie the spider as she gave her old friend a hug. "And, Dot," she said, turning to the pint-sized ant princess, "you must've grown a whole millimeter since last season!"

The ants had not seen their circus friends since last fall when, with the circus bugs' help, the ants had defeated Hopper, the grasshopper bully who had threatened the colony. Then the circus bugs had gone on tour with P.T. Flea's World's Greatest Circus. But they had promised to visit the colony the following season, and now here they were at last: Rosie, Slim the walking stick, Francis the male ladybug, Heimlich the butterfly, Manny the praying mantis and his moth assistant Gypsy, Dim the beetle, and Tuck and Roll the pill bugs! Even P.T. Flea, the circus owner himself, was there!

"Listen!" Flik said to the circus bugs once he had greeted them all. "Dot and I have a surprise for you. We've organized a variety show with a number of great acts!"

"Yeah," said Dot. "We figured that, as circus performers, you're always entertaining others. So today, we're going to entertain *you*!"

The circus bugs exchanged excited looks. Gypsy clapped her hands in delight. Heimlich flapped his tiny butterfly wings. Francis good-naturedly elbowed Slim in the side.

"Ouch!" cried Slim.

"Oops! Sorry, Slim," Francis replied. "So, Flik, when's curtain time?"

"Right away!" exclaimed Flik. He turned to Dot. "You gather the performers," he told her. "I'll organize the audience. Deal?"

"Deal!" Dot replied. She hurried off in the direction of the anthill while Flik led the circus bugs, along with a crowd of ant onlookers, over toward a makeshift stage he and Dot had constructed in the middle of a clearing.

Minutes later, Flik took his place onstage as the variety-show emcee. He had seated the circus bugs front and center, and the ants had filled in around them, also eager to watch the performances. Now all they needed were the performers.

Just then, Flik spotted Dot hurrying toward him with the stars of the show in tow: Queen Atta and her mother, a dozen or so ants from Dot's Blueberry troop, and three ant boys named Reed, Grub, and Jordy. Flik cleared his throat and began his introduction of the first act.

"Okay, everybody," Flik announced, "welcome to the First Ever Ant Colony Variety Show! Today's performance is dedicated to our special guests, the circus bugs!"

The audience clapped and cheered.

"Now, sit back, relax, and enjoy the musical stylings of Queen Atta and Princess Dot, singing 'High Hopes.' Come on, folks, let's give 'em a big hand!"

Flik clapped with the audience as he waited for Dot and Atta to take the stage. But when the performers did not appear, Flik rushed offstage to find Dot and Atta looking very anxious. "What's the matter?" he whispered to them.

Atta opened her mouth to reply, but no words came out.

"Atta's lost her voice," Dot explained. "She can't sing. We can't do our number."

Flik was flustered for a moment, but quickly regained his composure. "Okay, okay," he said. "We'll just move on to the second act."

Dot looked worriedly at Atta.

"What?" said Flik. "There's a problem with the second act?"

"Aphie has stage fright," Dot replied. Flik looked over at the Queen Mother and her trembling pet, Aphie, and saw that the second act was a lost cause, too.

"Third act?" Flik asked Dot hopefully.

Dot shook her head. "The captain of the Blueberry acrobatic team isn't here yet," she explained. "Without her, there's no one to top their pyramid."

Flik looked questioningly at Reed, Grub, and Jordy. "What about you, boys?" he asked them. "Ready to go on? Those jokes of yours will leave them rolling in the aisles!"

But the boys were hesitant. "We can't go out there *first*," said Reed.

"That crowd is not even warmed up," added Grub.

Flik sighed and dropped his head, feeling utterly defeated. "Well, that's our whole show, down the drain," he said with a shrug. "I guess I'll just have to go out there and tell them that our First Ever Ant Colony Variety Show is over . . . before it even began."

27

Flik turned to walk onstage, but found his way blocked—by the circus bugs!

"The crowd is getting restless," Francis said.

"Anything we can do to help?" Rosie asked gently.

Reluctantly, Flik explained the situation to his guests of honor. "Atta can't sing, Aphie has stage fright, the Blueberry acrobatic team captain didn't show, and our comedy act here won't go on without a warmed-up crowd."

The circus bugs just smiled. They were used to improvising when things didn't go as planned.

"The show must go on!" P.T. Flea exclaimed.

"Right!" cried Rosie. "Now, here's what we're going to do." The circus bugs pulled Flik and Dot into a huddle, and they made their game plan.

Then, lo and behold, the show *did* go on!

The first act delighted the crowd with the sweet sounds of Dot and Rosie, who, as it happened, knew all the words to "High Hopes."

The second act had the audience in stitches as Dim played the role of Aphie the aphid in the Queen Mother's amazing aphid act.

The third act wowed the spectators with the balance and agility of the Blueberry acrobatic team, who took on two honorary members, Tuck and Roll.

By the fourth act, the crowd was sufficiently warmed up, and Reed, Grub, and Jordy took the stage to amuse the audience with their best jokes.

Then, as the First Ever Ant Colony Variety Show came to a close, all the performers took a bow before a cheering crowd. Flik and Dot looked up and down the row of performers, and into the wings at the other circus bugs clapping for them, and they smiled. So the show hadn't turned out *exactly* the way they had planned it. But working together with the circus bugs toward a common goal—whether it was defeating grasshopper bullies or putting on a variety show—was just like old times. And that felt great!

DISNEY·PIXAR
MONSTERS, INC.
The Last Laugh

Ever since Monsters, Inc. had made the changeover from collecting scream energy to collecting laugh energy from human children, Mike Wazowski had gotten used to his reputation as the funniest monster in the company and number one in the laugh-collecting department.

"Feeling funny today?" Sulley asked Mike on the Laugh Floor one morning. Sulley was the president of Monsters, Inc. and Mike's best friend.

Mike smiled. "You bet! You wanna hear some of my new material? So this monster walks into a deli—"

Just then, a chorus of hysterical laughter filled the Laugh Floor, catching Mike off guard.

"Hey," said Mike, looking around to see where the laughter was coming from, "if you think that's good, wait 'til you hear the punch line!"

But Mike quickly realized that the laughter wasn't for him. Across the Laugh Floor, a group of employees stood guffawing around another monster. Mike turned to Sulley. "Who's the comedian?" he asked.

"You haven't met Stan, our newest recruit?" Sulley replied, looking surprised. "Come on. I'll introduce you."

Sulley led Mike across the room toward the group of employees.

"Good morning, Mr. Sullivan!" Stan said when he saw Sulley approaching.

Sulley extended a hand in greeting. "Please, Stan, call me Sulley," he replied. "Hey, there's someone I'd like you to meet." Sulley turned to Mike, who was standing at his side. "Mike Wazowski, this is Stanley Stanford. Stan just joined our laugh team yesterday," Sulley said to Mike. Then he turned to Stan. "And Mike here is our top Laugh Collector. He has been with us since we started collecting laugh energy," Sulley explained, "and long before that, too."

Mike and Stan shook hands as one of the can wranglers, Needleman, tapped Stan on the shoulder. "Mr. Stanford," he said eagerly, "tell them the joke you just told us." Needleman turned to Mike. "You've just gotta hear this one, Mr. Wazowski."

Stan seemed reluctant at first, so Mike encouraged him.

"Come on, Stan," said Mike, "let's hear it. I love a good laugh."

"Well, all right," Stan replied with a shrug. "I was just telling them about the time I met the Abominable Snowman and his mother. I said to him, 'Hey, Mr. Snowman, where's your mother from?' And he said, 'Alaska.' And I said, 'Hey, don't bother. I'll ask her myself!'"

All the employees burst out laughing all over again—everyone except Mike, who couldn't help feeling just a tiny bit *green* with envy. Who did this guy think he was, Mike thought, waltzing in there and stealing all the laughs, when it was he, Mike Wazowski, who had been there for so long, honing his craft, working hard for every giggle, guffaw, and chuckle?

Mike felt like his reputation as the number-one laugh-getter at Monsters, Inc. was being challenged! He had to step up and remind everyone who was king—king of laughs—before they all decided that Stan was funnier than he was!

"Hey, good one, Stan," Mike said when the laughter had died down. "But have you heard the one about the skeleton who decided not to go to the party?" All eyes turned to Mike as the crowd waited for the punch line: "He had no body to go with!" Mike exclaimed.

A wave of laughter crashed over Mike. He was back on top!

But Stan had another joke. "That's funny, Mike," he said. "Have you heard the one about the big elephant that wouldn't stop charging? The only way to stop him was to take away his credit card!"

Now everyone was laughing at Stan again. Mike's eye narrowed in determination as he called all of his best jokes to mind. No one could beat him in a joke showdown!

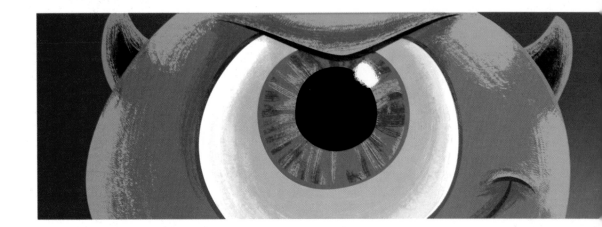

As the jokes came fast and furious, the employees formed a circle around the two jokesters.

"Did you hear the story about the oatmeal?" Mike said. "Aw, never mind. It was a lot of mush!"

"What do you call a chicken at the North Pole?" Stan said, posing a riddle. "Lost!"

"Anybody know the difference between a dancer and a duck?" Mike called out. "One dances Swan Lake, the other swims in it!"

"What is a monster's favorite play?" Stan asked the crowd. "*Romeo and Ghouliet!*"

Pretty soon, the crowd of employees was laughing so hard and so loud that they could barely hear the jokes. Yet the joke-off continued until—in a moment of panic—Mike completely blanked on all of his jokes! The harder he tried to think of a joke, the emptier his mind became! What would he do? What would he say? It was his turn, and the employees' laughter began to die down as they awaited Mike's next joke. As his anxiety grew, Mike began to jump up and down, hoping to jump-start his brain, but nothing was coming to him.

Then, in one of his panicky little jumps, Mike accidentally landed on the edge of a four-wheeled dolly that the employees used to move heavy things around the Laugh Floor.

"Waaaaaaah!" Mike cried as the dolly took off, rolling across the room and carrying him with it, completely off balance and out of control.

The employees watched as Mike careened wildly across the Laugh Floor. They fell down, paralyzed by laughter. When Mike landed in a pile of empty cardboard boxes, the joke-off was officially over, and Mike was the hands-down winner.

Sulley and Stan helped Mike out of the pile of boxes.

"You're a funny guy, Mike Wazowski," Stan said, giving Mike a pat on the back.

Mike smiled. Stan wasn't such a bad guy, after all. And with two hilarious monsters on the laugh team, thought Mike, just imagine all the laugh energy they could collect!

Still, Mike didn't want to let on that his dramatic exit had been an accident. So he put his arm around Stan's shoulders and offered him a piece of advice.

"If there's one thing I've learned over the years," said Mike, "it's never underestimate the power of slapstick comedy."

THE INCREDIBLES

Super Annoying!

Dash was bored. It was Saturday afternoon, and he had run out of things to do. He had already taken a twenty-mile run, cooled off with fifty laps over at the town pool, and chased the neighbor's dog around the block. But with Dash's Super speed, that had only killed about five minutes.

He was sitting in his messy bedroom on his unmade bed, wondering what to do, when his mother, Helen, walked past the doorway.

"You know, Dash," his mom said, stopping to poke her head into the room, "if you're looking for something to do, you could clean up your . . ." Before Helen had a chance to finish, Dash raced around his room and cleaned it up.

"I'm still bored," Dash said with a groan.

"Well, you could . . . read a book," Helen said as she left his room.

That's boring, thought Dash.

Just then, the telephone rang. Violet raced out of her bedroom to get it, and Dash's eyes zeroed in on her. Target spotted.

"Now this will be fun," he said to himself. Dash stopped in Violet's doorway. A sly grin spread slowly across his face.

Dash's eyes darted back and forth between Violet's bedroom and the kitchen, making sure his sister wasn't looking. Then he hurried into her room in search of a good place to hide.

Five minutes later, Violet came back into her room and closed the door behind her. She started to cross to her bed, but halfway there she stopped in her tracks and looked around. Things were not as she had left them. The bedspread was upside down. The lampshade on her lamp was missing; her books had been moved around; and the posters that hung around her mirror were rearranged.

"Mom! Dash rearranged all of my stuff!" Violet yelled.

As Helen walked down the hall, a breeze whipped through Violet's room. Helen looked inside.

"It looks fine to me, honey. Your brother is reading a book in his room. Now I've got to get dinner ready," she said.

Violet's eyes scanned the room. Everything was back in place.

Then her eyes fell on the closet door, which stood ajar. She went over to the door and threw it open.

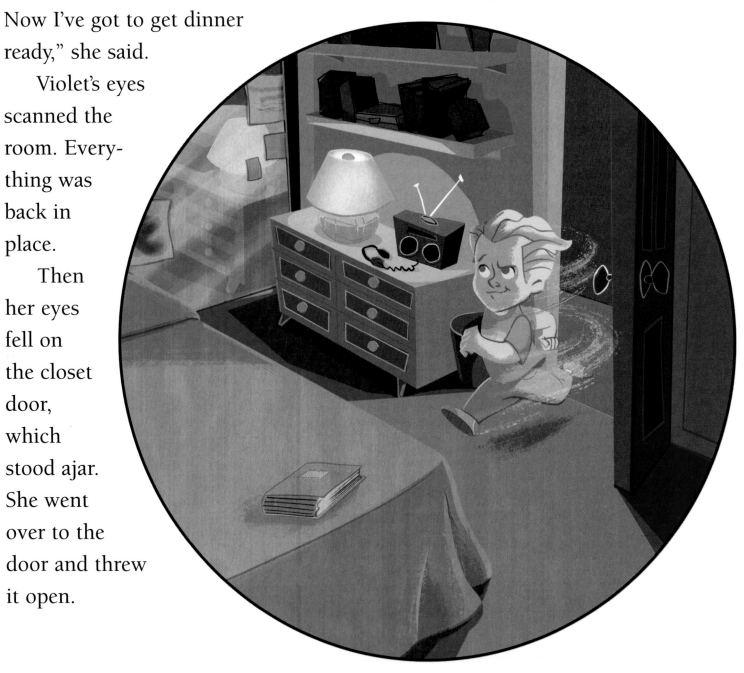

"Dash!" Violet exclaimed, pushing some clothes aside to find her brother crouched behind them. "Get out of here, you little insect!"

Dash jumped up wearing some of Violet's clothes. "Look at me. I'm Violet. I'm in love with Tony Rydinger."

Violet reached in, grabbed Dash by one arm, and pulled him out of the closet. Then she dragged him across the room and pushed him out into the hall.

"Stay out of my room!" Violet yelled, slamming the door behind her brother.

Dash dropped the clothes in the hall, sped out the front door of the house, and snuck around to the backyard. He stood on tiptoe to peer in through Violet's bedroom window. Violet hadn't even had time to cross the room and sit down on her bed before she spotted her little brother staring in at her.

"Yoo-hoo, Violet!" Dash called to her in a sickly-sweet, singsong voice as he threw her a dainty wave.

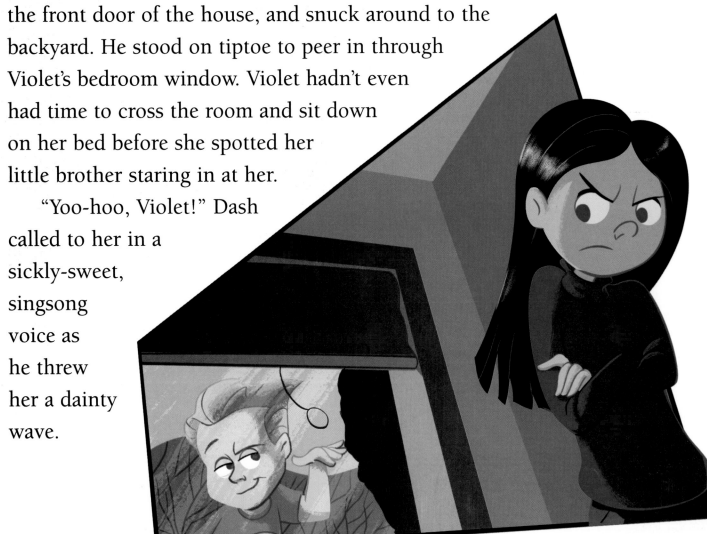

Violet rushed to the window and pulled down the shade.

As she sat on her bed, she felt something under her. "Aaaahhh!" she screamed.

"Forget to lock something?" Dash said, poking his head out from under the covers. Then he zoomed around and around—up onto the bed, down to the floor, around Violet—all at such Super speed that Violet couldn't even tell where he was at any given moment. All she saw was a blur flying around her room, kicking up a whirlwind of papers and blowing pictures off her mirror.

"Dash!" Violet shouted. "Knock it off!"

But Dash only came to a halt when he spotted Violet's diary, which had been blown off a bookshelf and had fallen open on her bed.

"Ooooh," Dash said, picking up the diary and eyeing it excitedly. "What have we here? Oh . . . poetry." Dash continued in a fake English accent. "'I love Tony. He dost the cutest. Shall I compare him to a . . .'"

That was it. Violet had had just about enough of Dash. "Give me that back!" she yelled.

Dash tried to race out of the room, but using her Super power, Violet threw a force field in front of the door. Dash ran into it head on and was knocked to the floor. The diary fell out of his hand, and Violet quickly snatched it away. But before she knew it, the diary flew out of her hand in a sudden wind.

"'How dost I love thee?'" Dash read the diary from the other side of the room.

Violet turned invisible and lunged at Dash. "You are gonna get it!" she cried.

Dash and Violet continued to chase each other around Violet's room in a blur of Super powers. Suddenly, they heard their mom calling to them.

"Violet! Dash!" she cried. "Time for dinner!"

Dash froze. Then, in the blink of an eye, he zipped out through the bedroom door and down the hall to the kitchen table.

"Dash," Helen asked, "did you finish your book?"

Then Violet appeared at the table. Her hair was all frazzled.

"Nah," Dash replied. "I found something better to do."